PRO SPORTS SUPERSTARS

Superstars of WORLD SOCCER

by Todd Kortemeier

AMICUS HIGH INTEREST • AMICUS INK

Amicus High Interest and Amicus Ink
are imprints of Amicus
P.O. Box 1329, Mankato, MN 56002
www.amicuspublishing.us

Copyright © 2017. International copyright reserved in all countries. No part of this book may be reproduced in any form without written permission from the publisher.

Library of Congress Cataloging-in-Publication Data
Names: Kortemeier, Todd, 1986-
Title: Superstars of world soccer / by Todd Kortemeier.
Description: Mankato, MN : Amicus High Interest, [2016] | Series: Pro sports superstars |
Includes index. | Audience: Grades: K to Grade 3.
Identifiers: LCCN 2015034790 (print) | LCCN 2015046153 (ebook) |
 ISBN 9781607539421 (hardcover) |
 ISBN 9781681510323 (pdf ebook) |
 ISBN 9781681521077 (paperback)
Subjects: LCSH: Soccer players--Biography--Juvenile literature.
Classification: LCC GV942.7.A1 K67 2016 (print) | LCC GV942.7.A1 (ebook) | DDC 796.3340922--dc23
LC record available at http://lccn.loc.gov/2015034790

Photo Credits: Kevin C. Cox/Getty Images, cover; Jorge Saenz/AP Images, 2, 17; Felipe Dana/AP Images, 5; Sven Simon/picture-alliance/dpa/AP Images, 6–7; Bullit Marquez/AP Images, 8; Andres Kudacki/AP Images, 10–11; Marcio Jose Sanchez/AP Images, 12–13; Manu Fernandez/AP Images, 14–15; Brynn Anderson/AP Images, 18–19; Frank Mattia/Cal Sports Media/AP Images, 21, 22

Produced for Amicus by The Peterson Publishing Company and Red Line Editorial.

Editor Arnold Ringstad
Designer Becky Daum

Printed in the United States of America
North Mankato, MN

HC 10 9 8 7 6 5 4 3 2 1
PB 10 9 8 7 6 5 4 3 2 1

TABLE OF CONTENTS

The World's Game	4
Pelé	6
David Beckham	8
Cristiano Ronaldo	10
Marta	12
Lionel Messi	14
James Rodriguez	16
Alex Morgan	18
Carli Lloyd	20
World Soccer Fast Facts	22
Words to Know	23
Learn More	24
Index	24

THE WORLD'S GAME

Soccer is the world's most popular sport. Players run across the field. They kick amazing shots. **Goalies** dive for saves. There are many soccer stars. Here are some of the best.

PELÉ

People call Pelé the best soccer player ever. He scored more than 1,000 goals. Teams could not stop him. Pelé helped Brazil win the **FIFA World Cup** in 1958. He is a hero in Brazil.

DAVID BECKHAM

David Beckham made great **free kicks**. He played for many big teams. Beckham played for England in three World Cups. The last was in 2006.

Beckham signed with a pro team at age 14.

CRISTIANO RONALDO

Cristiano Ronaldo became a pro in 2003. He scores from all over the field. He is very fast. He was named best player in the world in 2014.

MARTA

Marta is one of the best soccer players ever. She won the **player of the year** award five times. Marta scores many goals. She was the top scorer at the 2007 Women's World Cup. Marta wears the number 10 on her jersey.

Marta has played for teams in Brazil, Sweden, and the United States.

LIONEL MESSI

Lionel Messi has been named player of the year four times. Many think he is today's top player. In 2012, he scored 91 goals in pro games. It was the most ever in one year.

JAMES RODRIGUEZ

James Rodriguez is a young star. He joined the team Real Madrid in 2014. His speed helps him get to the ball. Powerful kicks help him score.

Rodriguez is one of the highest paid soccer players ever.

ALEX MORGAN

Alex Morgan is a US soccer star. She plays in the **NWSL**. She also won an **Olympic** gold medal in 2012. She helped the US team beat Japan.

CARLI LLOYD

Carli Lloyd helped the US team win the 2015 Women's World Cup. She scored in four straight games. Lloyd was named the tournament's best player.

Lloyd also has two Olympic gold medals.

WORLD SOCCER FAST FACTS

FIFA Founded: 1904

First World Cup: 1930

Most World Cup Wins: 5, Brazil

Most Women's World Cup Wins: 3, United States

Most Career Goals (all competitions): 1,279, Pelé (1956–1977)

WORDS TO KNOW

FIFA – the organization in charge of soccer around the world; its name means Fédération Internationale de Football Association, which is French for "International Federation of Association Football"

free kick – a play in soccer that allows one team to kick the ball with no opposing players nearby

goalie – a player who tries to stop the ball from going into the goal

NWSL – the National Women's Soccer League, the top US women's soccer league

Olympics – an international sports competition

player of the year – an award given to the top male and female player each year

World Cup – the world championship tournament for international soccer teams; it is held every four years

LEARN MORE

Books
Hoena, Blake. *Everything Soccer*. Washington, DC: National Geographic Society, 2014.

Jökulsson, Illugi. *Stars of Women's Soccer*. New York: Abbeville Press Publishers, 2015.

Websites
ESPN FC
http://www.espnfc.us
This website features the latest news about teams, players, and matches.

FIFA
http://www.fifa.com
The official FIFA website includes information about the history of every World Cup.

INDEX

Beckham, David, 9

FIFA World Cup, 7, 9

goals, 7, 13, 14, 20

Lloyd, Carli, 20

Marta, 13
Messi, Lionel, 14
Morgan, Alex, 19

Olympics, 19, 20

Pelé, 7

Rodriguez, James, 16
Ronaldo, Cristiano, 10

Women's World Cup, 13, 20